CHANGE-A-LOT COOLEST RULEST IN NAPPI

Library of Congress Cataloging-in-Publication Data
Cole, Babette. King Change-a-lot.
Summary: With the help of a genie from his potty,
the infant son of an ineffectual king and queen makes
some sweeping changes in his kingdom and improves
the lot of everyone. [1. Kings, queens, rulers,
etc.—Fiction. 2. Babies—Fiction] I. Title.
PZ7.C6734Ki 1989 [E]   88-18397
ISBN 0-399-21670-7

King Change-a-lot
by
Babette Cole

G. P. Putnam's Sons · New York

Prince Change-a-lot was fed up with being treated like a baby.

His parents, King and Queen Spend-fortune, were doing a bad job of running the kingdom and everyone was complaining.

They spent the people's taxes on silly parties and expensive clothes.

They hardly ever saw Prince Change-a-lot, who was looked after by Miss Grumpbladder, the court nanny.

There was a plot to blow up the government offices
because nobody was governing properly . . .

and big hairy giants were kicking down castles left, right and center . . .

. . . and the bad fairies were cooking up some rotten spells,

so the good fairies had to go on strike!

To make matters worse, the dragons were rampaging all over the place, and flying off with maidens belonging to the neighboring kingdoms.

There was a plague of disgusting blubber worms who were eating all the crops.

But the King and Queen did not want to hear anything so distasteful.

Nor did they want to hear about the bad behavior
in the kingdom's boring old schools.

"I'd change a few things around here," said Prince Change-a-lot, "if only I could talk like a grown-up."

One day he saw the court magician
making a genie appear by rubbing a pot.
The genie could grant wishes.

He tried the same trick on his own potty and out came a baby genie who could understand baby language!

"Leave it all up to me,"
said the baby genie.

BLAH BLAH BLAH BLAH

The baby genie whizzed over
Prince Change-a-lot . . .

The baby genie whizzed over Change-a-lot's parents.

Two minutes later they were behaving like the worst kinds of babies themselves!

The baby genie whizzed back
into the potty.
"OK," said Prince Change-a-
lot, "I'm King now."

The first thing he did was to give his
parents to Nanny Grumpbladder.

Then he turned the government offices into a gigantic
fun-fair so that nobody wanted to blow it up.

It had a rubber disco castle for the giants to bounce on, which was far more fun and less painful than kicking down real castles.

King Change-a-lot had all the bad fairies locked up so that the good fairies could get back to work.

He gave the dragons video games to play so that they would stay at home.

The neighbors were pleased to pay the new king for keeping the dragons away.

With the money he bought truckloads of candies and cakes . . .

. . . which he fed to the disgusting blubber worms,
who ate so much candy they just exploded!

¡BANG!

Finally, he closed down all the boring old schools because he didn't want to go to one . . .

. . . and he didn't want to send his parents to one either!

King Change-a-lot lived to be
a very clever and popular monarch . . .

. . . with the help of his potty!